To Mom, my light in the dark

• A NOTE ON THE ART •

BENJAMIN HARKNESS

These illustrations were created wearing a virtual reality headset. Each page is meticulously sculpted inside a VR "workspace" in much the same way I would sculpt with real clay. That "sculpture" is then imported into another program where photographed textures of my real clay are applied, fingerprints and all. I then add in lighting—in a similar way to how sunlight illuminates real clay—and create a still render or photograph. I bring that photograph into Photoshop where I apply the final color that you see on the pages of the story—blue for Wolfboy and purple for the Grumble Monster!

BLOOMSBURY CHILDREN'S BOOKS
Bloomsbury Publishing Inc., part of Bloomsbury Publishing Plc
1385 Broadway, New York, NY 10018

BLOOMSBURY, BLOOMSBURY CHILDREN'S BOOKS, and the Diana logo
are trademarks of Bloomsbury Publishing Plc

First published in the United States of America in July 2023
by Bloomsbury Children's Books

Text and illustrations copyright © 2023 by Andy Harkness

Bloomsbury books may be purchased for business or promotional use.
For information on bulk purchases please contact Macmillan Corporate and Premium Sales
Department at specialmarkets@macmillan.com

Library of Congress Cataloging-in-Publication Data
Names: Harkness, Andy, author, illustrator.
Title: Wolfboy is scared / by Andy Harkness.
Description: New York : Bloomsbury, 2023. | Series: Wolfboy ; book 2 |
Summary: Even though Wolfboy claims he is not afraid of the Grumble Monster,
things start to get spooky when he walks through the monster's lair with his
rabbit friends.
Identifiers: LCCN 2022042137 (print) | LCCN 2022042138 (e-book)
ISBN 978-1-5476-0445-6 (hardcover)
ISBN 978-1-5476-0446-3 (e-pub) • ISBN 978-1-5476-0447-0 (ePDF)
Subjects: CYAC: Fear—Fiction. | Wolves—Fiction. | Rabbits—Fiction. | Monsters—Fiction.
Classification: LCC PZ7.1.H3713 Wq 2023 (print) | LCC PZ7.1.H3713 (e-book) | DDC [E]--dc23
LC record available at https://lccn.loc.gov/2022042137

Typeset in Niramit SemiBold and Londrina
Book design by John Candell
Printed in China by Leo Paper Products, Heshan, Guangdong
10 9 8 7 6 5 4 3 2 1

To find out more about our authors and books visit www.bloomsbury.com
and sign up for our newsletters.

WOLFB☾Y
IS SCARED

ANDY HARKNESS

BLOOMSBURY
CHILDREN'S BOOKS
NEW YORK LONDON OXFORD NEW DELHI SYDNEY

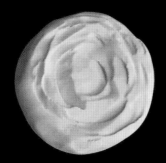

Wolfboy was having so much fun.
He had played all night with his
rabbit friends.

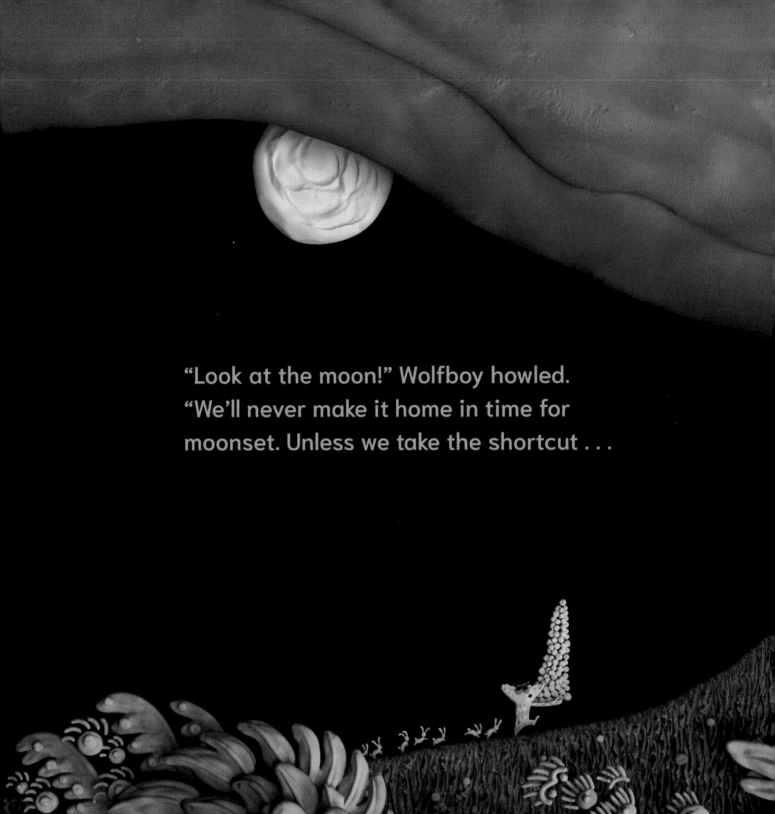

"Look at the moon!" Wolfboy howled.
"We'll never make it home in time for
moonset. Unless we take the shortcut . . .

. . . through the lair of the **GRUMBLE MONSTER.**"
Wolfboy shivered.

"It's ok to be scared," the rabbits giggled.

"I'M NOT SCARED!" Wolfboy huffed.
"But you go first, rabbits. I'll make sure the
monster doesn't sneak up behind us."

Trees creaked and
cracked as they
quietly crept.

"Are those **MOLDY
MONSTER TOES**?"

"Those are mossy
roots, Wolfboy."

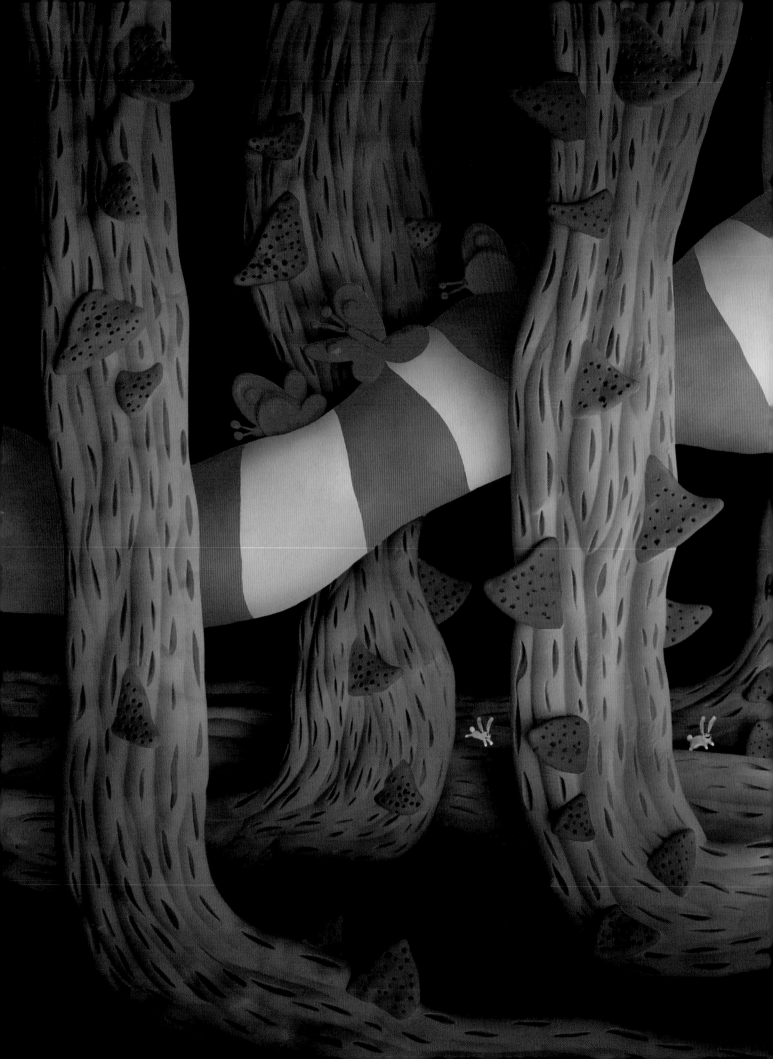

"Is that a **SPIKY MONSTER TAIL**?"

"It's a bramble vine, Wolfboy."

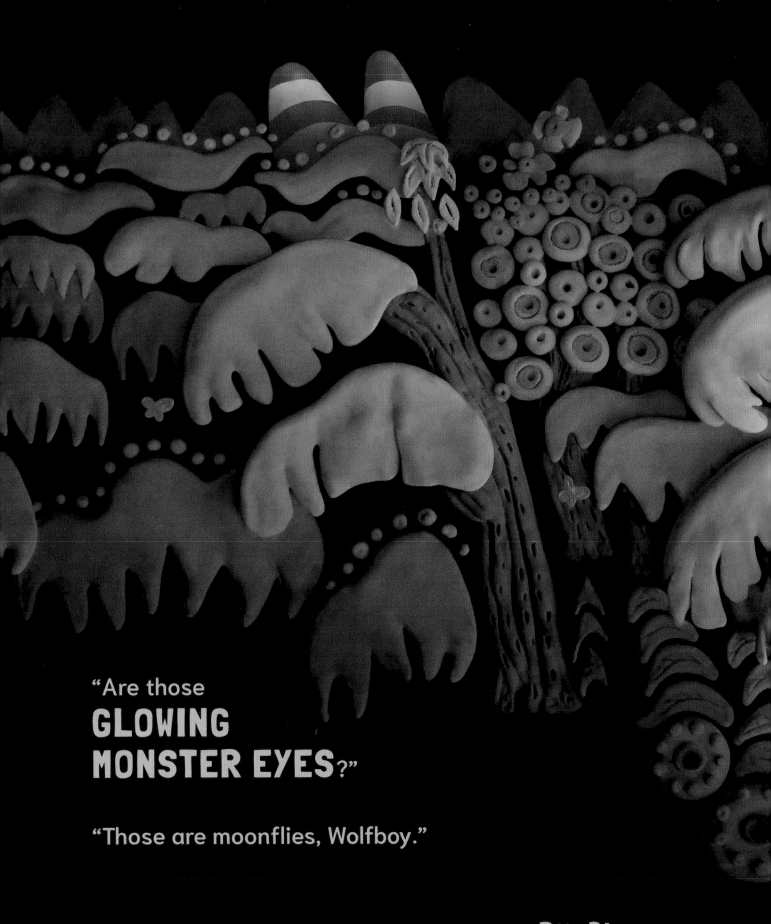

"Are those
**GLOWING
MONSTER EYES**?"

"Those are moonflies, Wolfboy."

Suddenly, they heard a low **GRUMBLE**.
"What was that?" Wolfboy whispered.

The **GRUMBLE** grew louder.
Wolfboy jumped behind the rabbits.
He covered his eyes and peeked
through his paws.

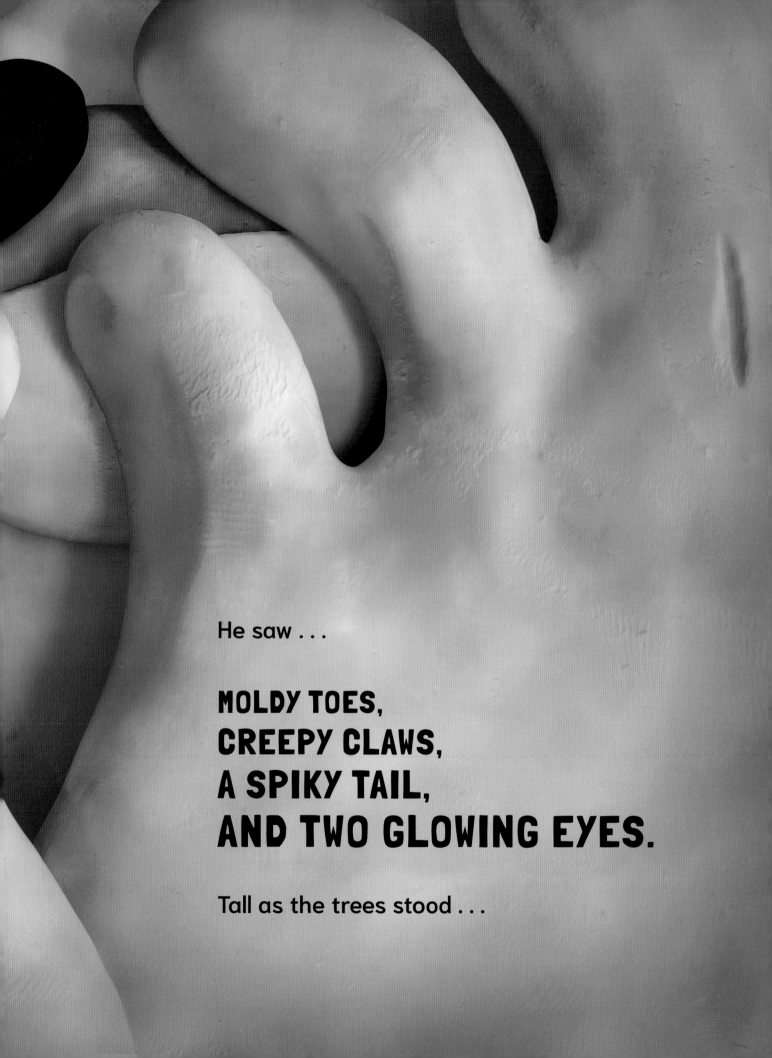

He saw . . .

**MOLDY TOES,
CREEPY CLAWS,
A SPIKY TAIL,
AND TWO GLOWING EYES.**

Tall as the trees stood . . .

. . . THE GRUMBLE MONSTER!

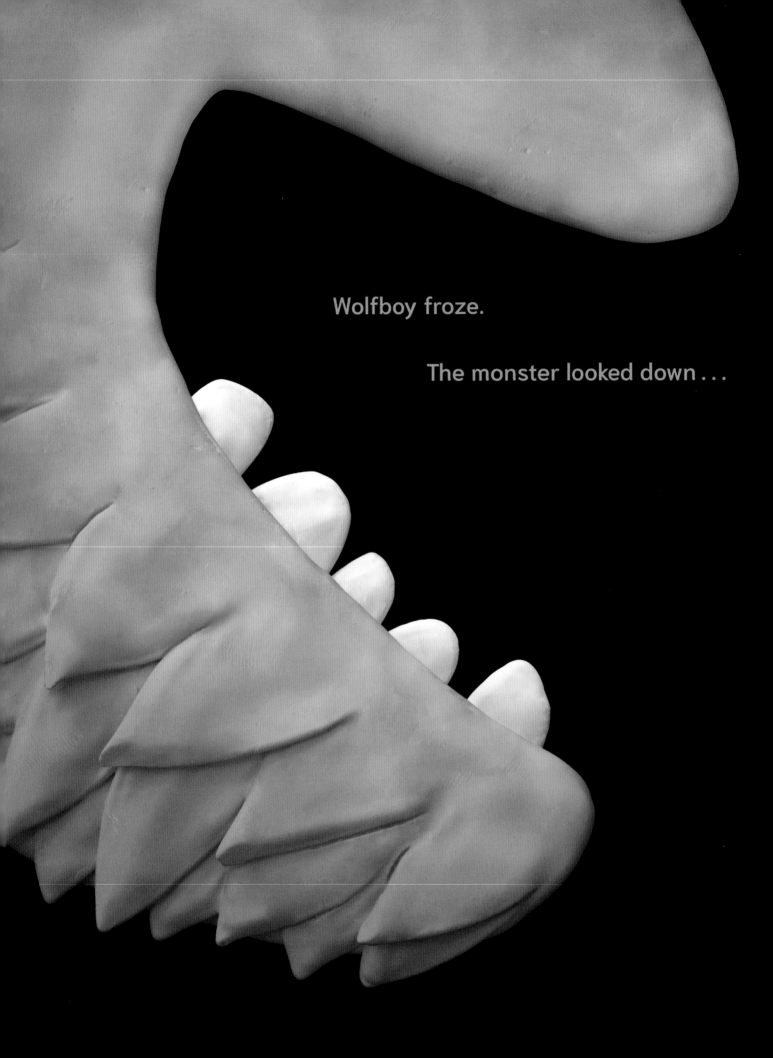

Wolfboy froze.

The monster looked down . . .

Leaned in . . .

Opened his mouth, and said . . .

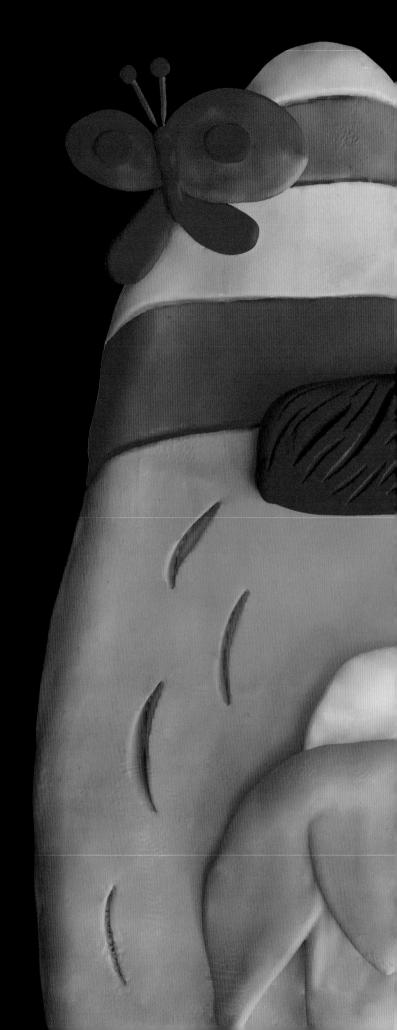

"May I have some moonberries? My tum is **GRUMBLING**."

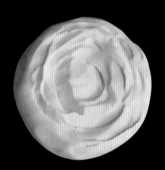

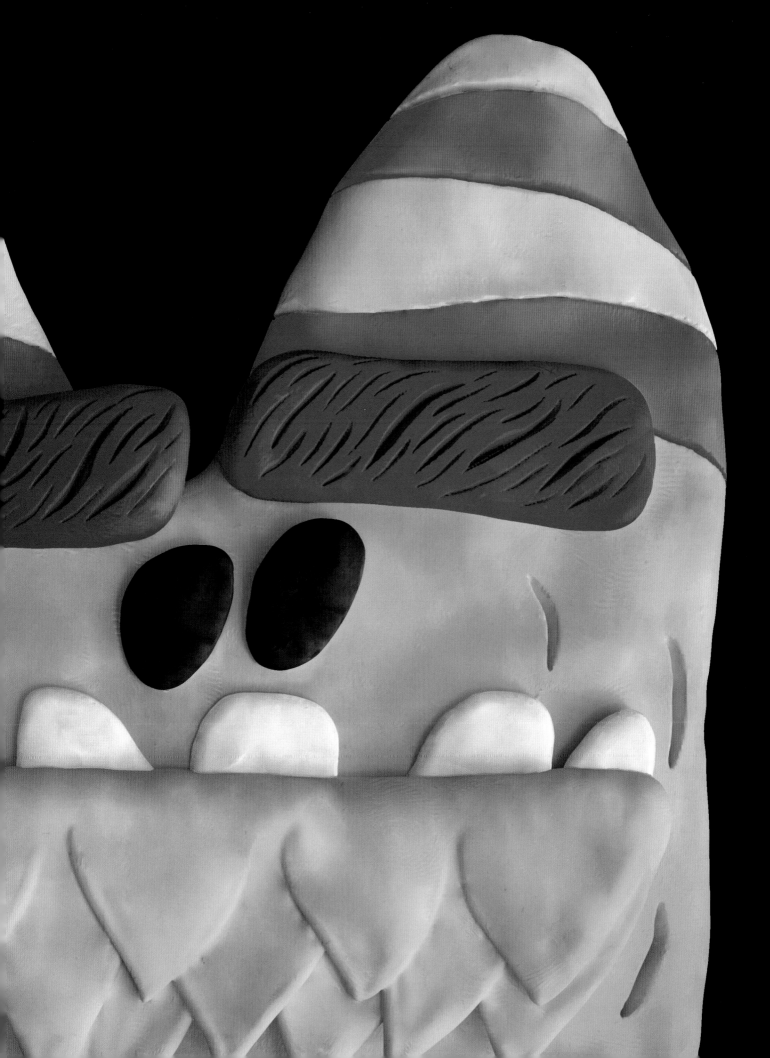

"That was your tummy?" Wolfboy gulped. "I know how you feel. Here, you can have all of them."

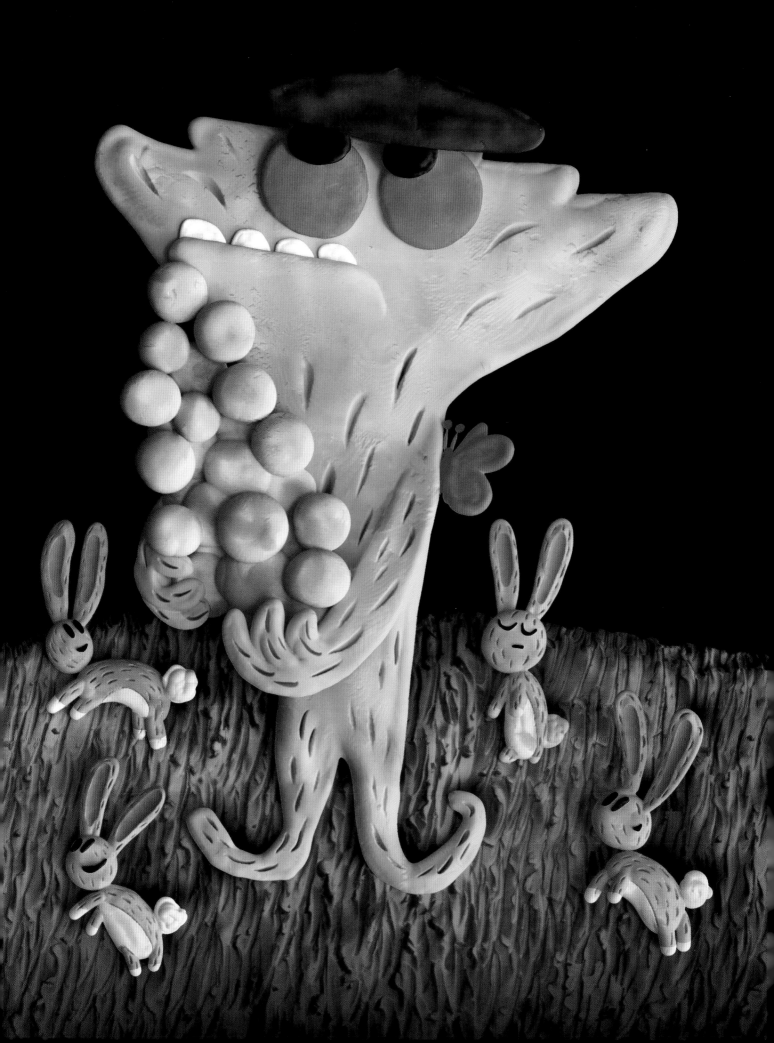

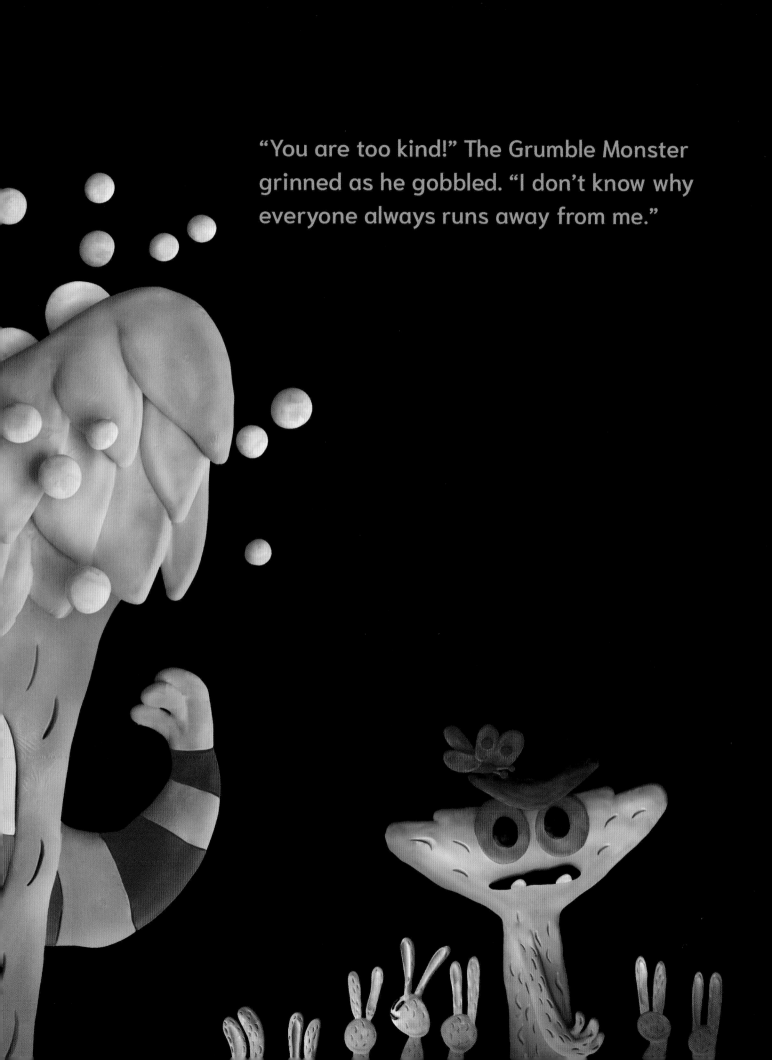

"You are too kind!" The Grumble Monster grinned as he gobbled. "I don't know why everyone always runs away from me."

The Grumble Monster
smiled and rubbed his eyes.

"Thank you," he said sleepily.
Soon, the forest shook from
his rumbling snores.

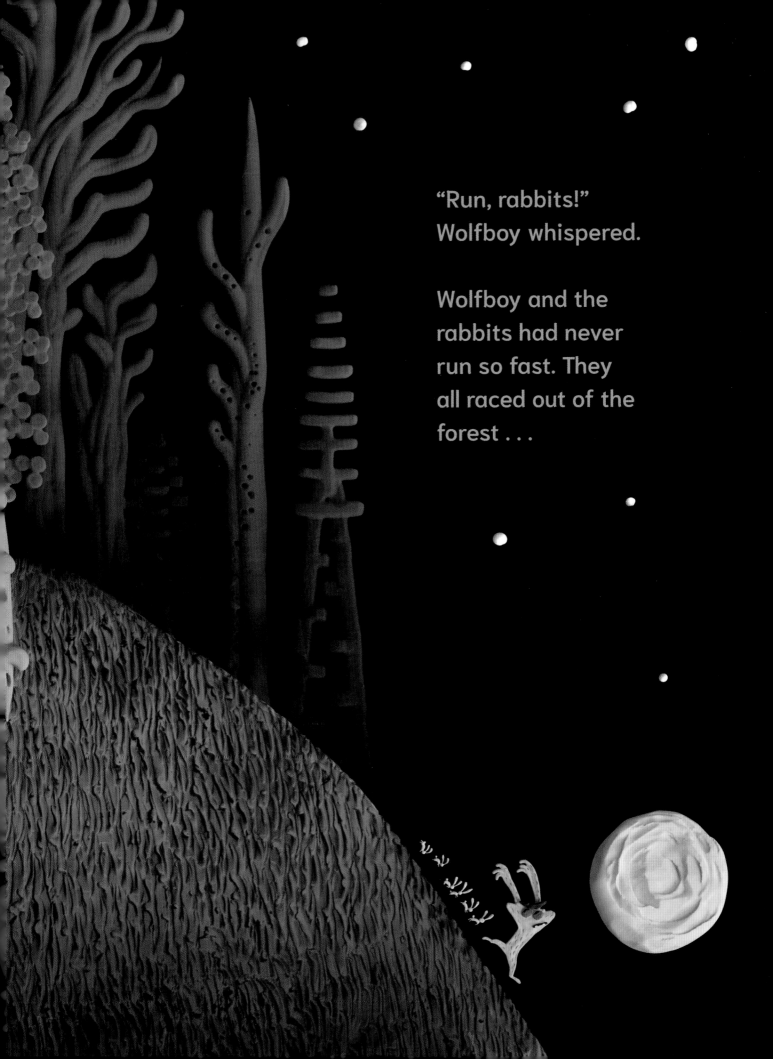

"Run, rabbits!"
Wolfboy whispered.

Wolfboy and the
rabbits had never
run so fast. They
all raced out of the
forest . . .

... and made it home just in time
to watch the moonset.